This book is to be returned on or before the last date stamped below.

D0726635

■Coventry City Libraries
Schools' Library Service

4 3 3 9 5 0 1 0 0 3 0 9 8 4 4 2 7 7 2 6 0 1 2

Bishop Ullathorne RC School

00010559

Also by William Mayne

Earthfasts
Cradlefasts
Candlefasts
Midnight Fair
A Swarm in May
Over the Hills and Far Away
Ravensgill
The Worm in the Well

and for younger readers:

Imogen and the Ark
Captain Ming and the Mermaid

*Other Silver titles available from
Hodder Children's Books*

The Shamer's Daughter
The Shamer's Signet
Lene Kaaberbol

The Oracle
Catherine Fisher

Carabas
Clementine
Sophie Masson

the ANIMAL GARDEN

WILLIAM MAYNE

Hodder
Children's
Books

A division of Hodder Headline Limited

Copyright © 2003 William Mayne

First published in Great Britain in 2003
by Hodder Children's Books
as part of the Hodder Silver Series

The right of William Mayne to be identified as the Author
of the Work has been asserted by him in accordance with the
Copyright, Designs and Patents Act 1988.

10 9 8 7 6 5 4 3 2 1

All rights reserved. No part of this publication may be
reproduced, stored in a retrieval system, or transmitted,
in any form or by any means without the prior written
permission of the publisher, nor be otherwise circulated
in any form of binding or cover other than that in which
it is published and without a similar condition being
imposed on the subsequent purchaser.

All characters in this publication are fictitious and any resemblance
to real persons, living or dead, is purely coincidental.

A Catalogue record for this book is available
from the British Library

ISBN 0 340 85425 1

Typeset by Avon Dataset Ltd, Bidford-on-Avon, Warks

Printed and bound in Great Britain by
Clays Ltd, St Ives plc

Hodder Children's Books
a division of Hodder Headline Limited
338 Euston Road
London NW1 3BH

COVENTRY SCHOOLS LIBRARY SERVICE

03-Apr-03	JF
PETERS	

Sonnet

O lovely O most charming pug
Thy gracefull air and heavenly mug
The beauties of his mind do shine
And every bit is shaped so fine
Your very tail is most devine
Your teeth is whiter than the snow
You are a great buck & a bow
Your eyes are of so fine a shape
More like a Christains than an ape
His cheeks is like the roses blume
Your hair is like the ravens plume
His noses cast is of the roman
He is a very pretty weoman
I could not get a rhyme for roman
And was obliged to call it weoman

Marjory Fleming, Kirkaldy, 1803–1811

One

The hot street was empty. All the streets were empty. Nothing moved in them. In the buildings either side no one had lived or worked for a thousand years. Only the sun and the lizards had walked up and down every burning day of all those years.

Philip kicked a stone. It had long ago fallen from a wall, and had not moved since. Now it skittered along the paving stones until it hit a fallen block with sandy carving on it, and lay on its own black shadow. The animal face of the carving gazed at it, the only change it had seen in a lifetime.

The girl, Shanya, had hardly said a word all day. She had been very disagreeable ever since Philip had met her. Now she stood against a wall between two pillars and glared at him from that shelter. She had wrapped herself in her long robe and fastened her arms firmly

1

round her. She hated all this street and this place, and blamed Philip.

She had to, because no one else was there. Philip felt he should not have kicked the stone, because of the noise it made, like a whole building falling in all the silence round them.

This was a deserted city, dry and abandoned. Even the trees were almost dead, their leaves withered on their branches. Only the glaring sun visited these streets today with Philip and Shanya.

In some distant alley a bird, perhaps, made a noise, not a song, not a call. And did it take off on a rattling wing, or had another dry stone fallen on a baked cobble? Or had a scorpion called out?

She is blaming me for it all, Philip thought, looking sideways at Shanya, and not looking too, not wanting to be seen to do so. She is blaming me for something. But nothing has happened yet.

Of course, something had happened, not last night but the night before. The girl thought that was Philip's fault as well, he was sure. How could it be? He had been asleep. But Shanya had hated him from the very beginning.

Somewhere among the buildings there were footsteps, walking, quick and light.

All at once Shanya hated him more. She twitched

with anger. Philip twitched with fright, and a cold shiver slithered up his back like a snake biting the back of his head so that his hair stood up cold in the heat.

Under the footsteps broken rubble moved and rattled. The footsteps came close, passed by out of sight, and went away. They were the footsteps of a ghost, Philip thought, not quite human, not precise enough. And Shanya's eyes moved in her head and she must think the same.

When the rustling rattle had gone Philip was more frightened of Shanya. She was still here, still angry, and bigger than he was. And he did not understand any of her thoughts, except the one about the ghost.

'We should go back to the camp,' he said. He had to start saying it twice, because the first time his lips would not move and his breath would not work.

Shanya looked at him. She looked right through him as if he was something that merely got in the way. She did not want to go back to the camp. She looked round her. She did not want to stay here either.

'We are lost,' said Philip, at last, because they were. There had been something very wrong at the camp. There was no help in the city, long dead inside its wall. There was no help in the mountains behind the city, and nothing to be found in the desert beyond the camp.

They were the only two people in a world that

everyone else had left. People don't die, thought Philip. Not me.

There was nothing in this place for them except shadows – was that how people became dead? First becoming all alone, and forgotten by the whole world. Or had the whole world been forgotten by itself, so there was nothing left but a dry city, itself already dead?

But something had walked by, though without noticing him or Shanya. If it had wanted it could have found them. But that might not be a good thing. Not everything in a ruined city between the barren mountain and the dry desert is fit to be met. Perhaps it was better it had not met them.

'Where are they?' said Shanya. She expected him to know and he did not. Shanya was like the desert herself, asking a question then shrivelling you dry if you answered. But he tried.

'Perhaps that was one of them,' he said. 'Walking by.'

'You did not call out,' said Shanya. 'It was an animal. You know it was an animal.'

Neither of them dared to mention ghosts.

Neither of them could imagine anything without dread.

Philip was not listening. He had a sudden feeling of comfort, and of being at home, among friends. He did

4

not understand why such a feeling had come to him, but it was there, complete and firm.

He knew he was safe and that he did not have to worry about anything more.

The feeling went away as soon as he knew why it had come. In fact the scent of wood smoke had come into his nose and reminded him of home and shelter and family.

And, after all, the feeling of safety and being found did not quite go away. Wood smoke among the decayed buildings meant that there was somewhere to go, something to search for, maybe not quite home, but at least another person in all the wilderness. Ghosts do not light fires. Nor do animals.

The fire also meant caution. It might not mean anything friendly and safe, however human.

Now Shanya was sniffing the air. She was sure everything was solved.

'There are people,' she said. 'They are going to cook. They will give us food. Let us go and find them. They will tell us what has been going on.'

'Slowly,' said Philip, which was sensible, but made her cross again.

'At once,' she said. 'Go and find them.'

They went together, tracking the invisible tags of smoke, finding them from empty corner to empty corner, losing them along the broken streets and hollow houses.

They came at last to the city wall and one of the abandoned watchtowers, and there the smoke was visible against the sky.

'They will be cooking,' said Shanya. 'I hope it will be something fit for me to eat. I expect you will eat anything.'

There was nothing cooking that they could eat. And nothing was offered to them. There was just a fire, in the roadway of a forgotten yellow ruin towards the middle of a long hot day.

Beside it, in the purple shadow, a small person was looking after the flames.

The small person turned its head to look at them. It was not a person but an animal of some sort, squatting down, holding a twig of kindling in its forepaws. The twig of wood was the spit for a small dead lizard.

On its head the small person wore some sort of golden hat, like a crown.

It calmly laid the stick against the fire. It was cooking the lizard.

Then it spoke to them.

How it spoke was terrifying in more than one way. What it said was perfectly clear but very alarming.

And worse than mere trifling things like danger.

Two

Two days ago Shanya had despised Philip, not only from the moment she and her ayah met him at the airport, but probably well before that. She had been practising it.

Philip's father's friend, Mr Jimrael, with a neat white suit and a neat brown face, had met him there an hour or so earlier, talking very kindly. 'How is the good Doctor Fleming?' he had asked, meaning Philip's scientist father.

They had a drink. 'You will enjoy yourself at the camp for a day or so,' he said. 'Interesting work has taken place, and Senjal Rhamid, who is working with your father, is such a very nice man, humorous and clever, from our own university here, you are sure to like him. Watch the arrivals board. Wet weather has delayed flights, and Jayid's rebels have made things worse, as usual. But Jayid is not very serious, no. We meet Senjal Rhamid's daughter and her ayah. It will be very good.'

It was not very good. When the plane at last arrived Mr Jimrael found the two ladies, and smiled at them, and was very nice to them, so full of politeness that Philip knew he would never learn it himself.

The two ladies were not at all delighted with Mr Jimrael. They looked at him as if he hardly existed. The ayah spoke only a little in a mean, sharp, voice.

'Here we have too many people,' she said. 'You should meet us more privately.'

'The airport is very public, yes,' said Mr Jimrael, 'but it is where we are bound to be, coming by aeroplane, yourselves, Philip, and indeed myself.'

The girl, a year or two older than Philip, was called Shanya. She and the ayah looked at Philip as if he did not exist at all. They would not sit down, they would not take a drink. They let Mr Jimrael collect their luggage, take it to a taxi, and put them in it.

'Pull down the blinds,' said the ayah. 'We are being seen by all sorts and sundries, and even soldiers.'

The girl sat in one corner and looked straight ahead. The ayah sat in the middle with her bag and a basket on the empty seat beside her. Mr Jimrael had to move them three times before she let Philip sit down. Mr Jimrael sat in front.

At the railway station Mr Jimrael went on being nice, but stopped being able to talk. At the very last, when he had found the right train and put them on it, he cleared his throat, held Philip back for a moment, and said, 'It is a side of Senjal Rhamid I do not know, that little girl of his. I will think of you in their disagreeable company if that will help you survive.'

The ayah spoke in her nasty voice as she settled down, trying not to thank Mr Jimrael. She wanted to blame him for the railway cushions. Mr Jimrael stepped back and put his hands together. The train left. The girl spoke to Philip.

'We think Mr Jimrael is a shopkeeper,' she said. 'He is that sort. My father is a professor, and my ayah the daughter of a prince.'

So that was that. Philip and his father and his father's friend were not good enough. Shanya wrapped her long dress round her and looked the other way.

Philip looked from the window and wished he was back at school. But at the end of this journey Dad would be waiting in a Land Rover, for the long trek to the camp.

Instead of taking four hours, the journey took seven. Night was beginning over flooded fields by the time

9

Dad found them. They waited on the train. Since the ayah was going further on to her home and not getting off here she would not get out herself or allow Shanya out. She grumbled.

There was more fuss, because Dad was not the right person. 'We are expecting the Professor Rhamid, doctor of science and doctor of philosophy, with a gold medal and head of the University department,' said the ayah in her grinding and complaining way. 'We are not expecting Mr Jimrael's friend.' She did not want to let Shanya go.

'Leave them on the train,' said Philip, quite fed up with both these women.

'Like that, is it?' said Dad. 'Come on, Phil, we'll be on our way. The ayah can explain to Rhamid if she meets him again.'

The train gave a great shake when its new engine ran into it. Shanya climbed down to the platform. The ayah at last handed down luggage. More people were trying to get into the compartment from the other side, so the ayah had that to think about as well. When the train got on its way the ayah signalled from the window until Shanya turned her back and ignored her.

She does it to everyone, Philip realized. They both do it to everybody.

Minutes later Shanya was wishing she had stayed on

the train, and saying so, and Dad was explaining that there had been no water at the camp in the desert to wash out the back of the Land Rover.

'Though there's plenty of it here,' he said, because there had been much rain and the streets were full of ponds. 'The animals were nervous in strange surroundings, and of course they are not quite house-trained. You'll get used to the smell.'

Shanya covered her nose with a loose sleeve. Philip breathed lightly. The animals had been very nervous, he thought.

The Land Rover jerked its way through town, crossed the swollen Pungal River by the wooden bridge, and began to go faster along the road beyond. The last houses moved away from the road, and there were fields. Shanya's sleeve fell away, her eyes closed, she leaned on Dad and went to sleep.

Even that was wrong, Philip thought, because leaning on his dad was his job.

He was asleep too, but not before the Land Rover had got beyond the floods, then the fields, and was starting on the desert. In places the desert was starting on the road, and there were sandy humps and bumps, waking him several times before he had closed his mind down.

Sudden silence from the end of the journey woke

11

him up in darkness. The driving lamps were all out and Dad was opening up the back of the vehicle to get the plastic water-cans. There was only the inside light, yellow as moonlight. Shanya was spread out, still asleep. Philip left her and went to help with the water-cans.

Someone carrying a bright solar lantern came through the sheds of the camp.

Light from the solar lantern showed up the bold pattern of his jacket, woven high up in the mountains but after a Scotch fashion. Philip could smell smoke on it from mountain fires.

'Now, who is this in my camp all of a sudden in the very middle of the night?' said that person.

'Dr Rhamid,' said Dad to Philip. 'Senjal, we are here.'

'And is there a daughter of mine?' asked Dr Rhamid, very jokingly. 'Is there such a thing?' He looked inside the cab and became serious. 'What is this, hey, what is this? Who is this you have brought? This is not a daughter. This is a pug, you have brought another pug. We have enough pugs already, dear Dr Fleming, yess, yess, far too many pugs.'

In the light of the solar lantern he held, his face was scowling fierce and angry.

Philip thought for a moment that he and Dad had

12

brought the wrong girl, that they might have to turn back, happily get rid of this disagreeable creature, and find someone more cheerful and amusing and pleased.

'Two pugs,' said Dad. 'What else?'

Three

But in the cab of the Land Rover Shanya woke up and was pleased at last to see someone respectable.

'It is the right one after all,' said Dr Rhamid, with a huge laugh. All the fuss and scowls had been his joke. 'Not a pug at all. Well, that is good. Now this is Philip? I hope you are getting on with my little girl. Now come in and we shall start the evening.'

He wrapped Shanya in a big hug, and then carried her. She pulled his moustache a little. In the sweeping, swinging, lantern light Philip thought she almost smiled, nearly looked pleased.

'You will get used to him,' said Dad.

'He's not like her,' said Philip. Dr Rhamid carried only his daughter. They were chatting in another language.

'One's enough in a small camp,' said Dad. 'He is

good company, but strong company, a great surgeon and a wonderful scientist.'

Dr Rhamid had been better than company or surgery or science. He had got ready a very big supper, and really cool drinks from the camp's ice-machine.

At first they sat outside in the darkness, with the stars pointing down at them sharp as needles, and the generator thudding to run lights and ice-machines. To one side was desert turning invisible as far as eyes could see. To the other side mountains began with a high rocky hill like a cliff blotting out the stars. When the solar lantern on the table was turned up all the flying things from all the stars came buzzing round their heads, and they had to go indoors. They turned on the ordinary camp electric lights. There would have been music, but the radio started to pick up bad interference and had to be switched off.

The radio telephone was full of static too.

'There are commotions,' said Dr Rhamid. 'But we are well away from all that.'

'In one of the towns there are riots,' said Dad. 'Or the satellite is too low.'

'There are rebels,' said Dr Rhamid. 'Jayid is starting a revolution, yess, but it will never work. My friend the President . . .'

'The President is his friend,' said Shanya. She was

15

proud of that, but seemed to have other thoughts too.

'He is not in danger,' said Dr Rhamid. 'The President is safe, yess.' He picked up a black beetle and let it crawl on his fingers, and bowed to it. 'Here is the President,' he said. 'And here is Jayid, the rebel,' and he picked up a brown beetle in the other hand. 'Jayid will fly away, so say Goodbye, Jayid.'

He made the brown beetle talk in a beetly way, and it was funnier for Shanya because she knew the words as well as the way they were said.

'It is just like him,' she said. 'The ayah has listened to him, it is how he speaks.'

The black beetle had to make his speech in a little, old, voice, full of long English words. That was the President, Philip knew.

When Dr Rhamid had finished his fun he put both beetles in one hand to throw them out into the night again. One of them bit him. He did not know which. 'Me, I do not matter,' he said. 'But the rascal must not bite the pugs.'

No one explained what a pug might be. Dad went on to say that neither Jayid's rebels nor the President's men would come out here and trouble them.

'The road goes nowhere else,' he said. 'It ends here. It was the road to the old city a thousand years ago. When the water dried up the people left. We came out

16

here to do our work, and this is the end of the work. When we have packed up we shall leave. We are waiting for transport and our Forest Rangers.'

'It is sad,' said Dr Rhamid. 'The President has sent the army to turn the water our way from the Pungal River beyond the mountains. But it has not happened.'

'The rains have started, but not here,' said Dad. 'They have not come here in a millennium. That is why the city died. It was full of temples and houses and palaces.'

'But up on the side of the mountain beyond there was a well that never failed,' said Dr Rhamid. 'It is in a place called The Animal Garden, where the king kept a zoo. It was famous, and we know all about it, yess. Only bones are left now, and hardly any trickle of water, but the walls still stand, and the pools where the water was, but none of the fountains. It was the city of the fountains. Oah, it is greatly sad that nothing is remaining for the pugs.'

Philip found that his eyes were closing. He was not hearing real words, but seeing imaginary pictures of dinosaurs in cages, prehistoric sharks in fountains. And what was a pug?

Dad picked him up and laid him on a bed. Philip tried to open his eyes while he took off his hot clothes, but they would not stay open. That part of him

17

was asleep. He heard Dad go outside and turn off the generator, so the light now ran from the batteries. It had already run out of Philip's eyes.

In his dreams he heard the wild and huge Rhamidosaur laughing in the squashy forest; but that was his head sinking into a pillow.

People got up early, he thought, waking a little, later on, hearing the Land Rover moving while the night was still dark. People walked about outside and called to one another. The Land Rover drove away, and Philip was asleep again.

He woke in quiet daylight. The sun was picking at the corners of the curtains and sending hot flames into the room. There was no sound. Dad had either not slept in his bed, or had made it when he got up.

They will be busy, Philip told himself. But it was very quiet. He got dressed and went to find Dad.

The room where they had had supper was still laid for that meal, with the dirty dishes among the food. The air was hot and stuffy. The electric light was still on, but the bulb had only a faint red glow in it. As he watched it faded to nothing.

They are busy, very busy, thought Philip. He looked outside. The hot desert sprang at him when he opened the door, spread empty and shimmering with heat.

Beyond this building there were others, closed up.

There were empty cages, smelling like the Land Rover last night. There were plastic water-cans lying about, water leaking from splits where vehicle tyres had crushed them and left tread-marks.

The batteries, like car batteries, that ran the light, were there. But the generator that charged them was no longer on its base. There were cut wires, and a splash of oil in the sand, and spilt battery acid had made the sand bubble.

There was a bad stale diesel smell. There was the spreading desert with its piercing silence.

There was no Land Rover. There was only Dad's wallet, his initials in gold on the corner of the green leather, open but empty, and lying in the track. Something had trodden on it, or perhaps even driven over it with the Land Rover.

There was no Dad.

Four

Philip picked the wallet up. There was nothing inside the folds of leather, not a coin, not a note, not a card. Philip went round the cabins of the camp again, looking for Dad, not wanting to call out. He did not want to find there was no answer.

He found no one outside, and did not want to knock on any doors if Dad and Dr Rhamid were busy with their work.

He wanted something to eat and drink, so he went back into the living quarters. They will be there waiting for me, he thought. One of them has gone in the Land Rover, but the other one will be here.

Shanya was in the room. She was looking at the table with disgust. She looked at Philip in the same way. She was dressed in her long clothes, but her hair had not been drawn back and strands of it hung across her face.

They made her look broken across, as well as out of patience.

'They are not outside,' said Philip.

'It is eleven o'clock,' said Shanya. 'No one has brought anything. Where are they?'

Philip did not know. He said so. Shanya knew it was his fault but found it hard to explain. She shook her head at him and pouted.

'We can have another supper,' said Philip. 'I am hungry and thirsty.'

'I need another plate,' said Shanya. 'How can I eat?'

There were no other plates. Philip thought she might wash one of those on the table, but Shanya had never washed a plate. 'Servants do that,' she said.

Philip filled a kettle. He lit the gas under it. Shanya wrinkled her nose at the smell. When Philip had shown her how, she managed to carry one plate, her own, from the table to the sink. She watched Philip scald his fingers in hot water, wash two plates, and dry them.

'I have never seen it happen,' she said.

'You get used to it,' said Philip.

It was a horrible meal. They ate cold rice with cold sauces on it. Philip made watery tea, after filling the kettle again with great difficulty from a water-can, spilling water over his feet and the floor.

They sat and waited a long time for someone to

come, but no one did. Philip felt more and more miserable, and a bit sick because of the meal. Shanya looked at him now and then, blaming him for everything, he supposed. Then she would turn away and look at the wall.

'They will be coming back soon,' said Philip, when the clock showed five. 'They will like a different meal.'

'All this must be sent away,' said Shanya. 'They should eat it in the kitchen places. But there are no servants. That is wrong, you know, because my father is a professor.'

Most of the food was full of flies now. Philip scraped dishes into the bucket outside the door. He stacked the empty dishes, boiled more water, and washed them all.

Shanya had never seen inside a cupboard of crockery that was used for anything. She only knew ornaments. She took the dry dishes and laid them on the table again. Someone would come and put food into them, she said.

No one came. Philip longed for ice cream, and Shanya looked as if the idea might please her. Philip found ice cream in the silent freezer. It had melted soft, but was cold in places.

That was their supper for the day. There was darkness next. But the solar lantern had been out in the sun all day and was full of light.

At midnight by the clock Shanya went to sleep on the couch. Philip lay under the table with his own pillow.

Shanya snored a little. Or perhaps she was crying. Philip could not tell and did not want to think about it in case he cried too. He had to hold his hands over his face to be certain not to. They smelt of washing-up.

By morning no one had come to the camp for them. There were no servants. Shanya was still outraged. There was only a hot room. They drank water that tasted mouldy, and ate some crust-hard bread, dipping it in a pond of melted butter from the dish. The butter had begun to taste old. Philip thought it smelt slightly of Shanya's ayah, but he said nothing.

'We shall walk back to the town,' said Shanya. 'To the railway. My ayah will come back on the train. We shall not get lost. There is only one road.'

'We shall go a little way,' said Philip. 'We should stay here. We cannot walk all the way to the town. They will come for us. Someone.'

'They have not,' said Shanya.

It is going to be bad luck for them when they do, Philip thought. She does not get any nicer.

The road led them towards the mountain, and then along just below it. Everything that side of the camp was mountain, all the way. After a time they saw houses beginning by the desert edge, then a long wall, and then archways in the wall.

'It is the city,' said Philip. 'Of course. It is the city with the water and the fountains.'

'We will find the right people,' said Shanya. 'Hotels. I know hotels.'

She tried to become happy, but she knew there would be no hotels. They both knew the city had died where it stood ten centuries ago, dry and empty, forgotten, unvisited. No hotels, no people.

Behind them the camp lay empty too. But it was like home now they had left it, a place they could go back to, where they lived.

'We'll go into the city,' said Philip. 'And then come out.'

'And go down there again,' said Shanya, looking at the camp. 'They will be back.'

They wandered up the slope into the high centre, where once there had been supermarkets, perhaps, or swimming pools, or the offices of airlines. Now there was no glass, no traffic. Only broken palaces.

There never had been offices of airlines, or McDonald's, or cars and wagons.

Philip kicked a stone. Shanya was angry that there were no shops or servants. She and Philip heard something walk in another street. They smelt smoke.

They came upon the small animal sitting over a fire, wearing a golden hat, a crown. It was cooking something, a small lizard, which it held on a stick.

'Good morning,' it said. 'Yess, very good. My name is Martin Fleming, Doctor Martin Fleming of the university here. Certainly.'

It said it was Philip's father. Those were its exact words. It said it in the style of Dr Rhamid. It had a whispery voice, and no lips along its doggy face.

Shanya fell down in a faint, giving a little cry of horror. Philip felt the world twitch for him, as if it had ended.

This was not danger. It was more than danger. It was impossible, but it was happening.

Five

Outside the city, beyond the walls, there was a sound that started the world again. Once, twice, three, four, five, six times, someone blew a motor horn or hooter.

Philip left Shanya where she lay. He was glad to have some other useful thing to do, because he had no idea how to deal with fainted persons.

He crossed the city wall to the outside edge. It was only a few paces to the crumbled battlement on the decayed edge of a high cliff. The cliff fell sometimes straight down, sometimes sloping in, sometimes leaning out. The ground at the bottom was far enough away to break you if you fell on it without having to be rock-strewn.

So with care not to fall down he looked out and over to one side towards the camp. Its little buildings and

26

tents were small, like more rocks on the edge of the sand desert.

It was not abandoned now. A visitor had come to it in a small elderly jeep and a trail of dust. It stopped by the cabins. A man got out and walked to the living quarters. He was on his way before the next half dozen calls from the horn reached Philip.

'Oah, that is Mister Jimrael,' said the creature by the fire, conversationally. 'One is asleep here,' it said, looking back at Shanya.

Shanya was beginning to sit up. She rubbed her forehead, which had grown cold on her.

'That is a monkey,' she said. 'Philip, put it back in its cage.'

'I have read the writing of your face,' said the animal to her. 'You are the mother of Doctor Rhamid. I am not a monkey any more. I am a pug. We are all brothers and sisters now. Mister Jimrael found us. We know who he is.'

Shanya took no notice of these remarks. Even most humans did not draw her attention. It seemed she knew a monkey when she saw one, and knew they did not speak or light fires or cook lizards, or know anything.

Philip knew that she was right, and that the animal was a dog-faced monkey with hands and a tail.

But it was possible for the monkey to be right as well.

27

He kept the word pug in mind. Dr Rhamid had used it already, so it was probably the right one.

Now there were other things to do. Mr Jimrael was walking about the camp looking at the ground, looking into the distance, pacing about, working something out. That was all very well, but did not seem to be finding Philip or Shanya, or either of their fathers.

'I will go and get Mr Jimrael,' said Philip. 'Quickly. He is getting into his jeep.'

'The mother will sit by the fire,' said the pug. Shanya was not frightened by the monkey, only offended. She did not want to run down to the camp. She decided to do what the monkey said, so long as everyone understood that she had really thought of it herself.

Philip went down through the ruins alone, taking a quick way through the rubble and fallen masonry. The monkey was talking to Shanya as he went down the first damaged alley.

'I am the king,' it was saying. 'My son has gone for firewood. My daughter is looking after the well. We need both. I cook a lizard.'

I have to leave it, Philip thought. I have to go away from the dream. Then he was all alone in the city gate, but with the dream still being remembered. He began to hurry down the littered roadway where it curved towards the camp half a mile away.

28

He looked back, and the city was all above him, the mountain behind that, and on the mountain the walled place with dry sticks of trees. That, he thought, will be The Animal Garden.

But Dr Rhamid had said there were no animals now. But I am one, Philip thought. I am the worst animal for this place. Or this is the worst place for this animal.

He heard the engine of the jeep grinding slowly, the tyres pushing among the loose stones on the road, or digging through sand to find the bottom of a gully.

Mr Jimrael was driving on the bits of road close to the jeep, watching them. He did not see Philip until he was twenty paces away.

'Oh,' said Mr Jimrael, putting his head out. 'You are all up here. I had been wondering. Your good father has not called me on the radio today or yesterday, no doubt something is wrong with it. I am following your walking track, two children up the road to the city of the fountains, but alas no fountains now. But alas too, where then is the Land Rover?'

'Oh Mr Jimrael, please come into the city and look at Shanya. She has fainted.'

'That is serious,' said Mr Jimrael.

'And a monkey is talking to her.'

'Oh, a pug,' said Mr Jimrael.

'Yes, a pug,' said Philip.

'Then that is all right,' said Mr Jimrael. 'But of course the pugs are not doctors, so I had better look at Shanya.'

'It will be quicker to walk,' said Philip, because Mr Jimrael was driving very slowly. Philip walked slowly beside the jeep.

'What I am puzzling,' said Mr Jimrael, 'is, where is the Land Rover and where is Dr Fleming; and Dr Rhamid, where is he? What has happened?'

'They are not here,' said Philip. 'And all we shall eat is a lizard cooked by the king.'

'The king?' said Mr Jimrael, shaking his head in a wise way. 'That is too bad, though of course I should not say so. Well, tut tutt.'

By then the jeep was at the city gate, where the arch threw a shadow.

'You have a town plan?' asked Mr Jimrael. It was a joke, but Philip thought that jokes were the wrong thing just now.

Mr Jimrael parked the jeep where it was, and got out.

'This way,' said Philip, leading Mr Jimrael up the shadows of the short cut.

'Be aware of snakes,' said Mr Jimrael.

Philip was more worried by pugs, talking and cooking and wearing the crown of a king.

When they came to the wall top Shanya was sitting up, proud as ever, not looking at her company. Her faintness had gone. There were now two pugs with her, the big one with the larger crown, and a smaller one with a smaller crown. The smaller one had a bad arm, and was cross.

When Mr Jimrael stepped into their view the big one stood up on his hind legs and then knelt down, which was hard for him.

'It is God,' he said. 'Mister Jimrael is God.'

'Oh dear,' said Mr Jimrael. 'What a naughty man is Dr Rhamid, it is a dark humour, how very mischievous.'

Six

One pug was on its knees to Mr Jimrael, another was jumping up and down to get his attention to its bleeding arm. Shanya was looking at the proceedings with great disdain. Mr Jimrael was surely not God. Thought if the pug called himself king that might be true: king of the pugs was nothing.

Philip was hot, hurried, thirsty, hungry, and bewildered. His throat coughed in the dry heat of the wall top when smoke curled into it. He moved away and sat down at the edge, high up, where the wind moved slightly and made one side of him cooler, and the other side hotter.

'She bit me,' the younger pug was saying in a strange unhappy whisper, holding out his arm. 'She is to keep the well, not the trees.'

'I am Doctor Martin Fleming,' said the king

pug. 'The good Doctor Fleming.'

He is using Dr Rhamid's voice, Philip thought, because Dr Rhamid taught him to speak and to think that.

Mr Jimrael was looking at the smaller pug's arm. 'Life does not always go according to plan,' he said. 'Who would think all this could happen, Shanya?'

Shanya did not speak. She got up and came to sit near Philip. 'He is a shopkeeper,' she said. 'He is not God. Is he?'

'I do not think so,' said Mr Jimrael. 'But who can tell? It is Senjal's joke, a greatly humorous man is Dr Rhamid, oh dear.'

Then he was cuddling the younger pug in a businesslike way until it forgot its hurt arm. It went to sit beside the king.

'God,' said the king, talking to a friend.

'Yes, king,' said Mr Jimrael, politely not minding that he was God.

'It is not very much water,' said the king.

'And her biting me,' said the young pug, remembering his arm again, snapping his teeth. He had long teeth.

'It is here,' said the king, getting up from his fire and leading the way. He walked on all fours. Most kings walk on their hind legs.

'You will come?' said Mr Jimrael to Philip and Shanya. 'It is better.'

They followed the king through the ruins. There were houses here where other pugs lived. Pugs sat in doorways and looked after their babies. Pugs called out in pug language to the king. Others shouted Hello, or Goodbye, mostly in pug language. But some of them knew words.

'It is God,' said the king. 'He will make the water wet again.'

The water was dry at the pool in the city. The king put down his cupped hands and lifted them up full of nothing for Mr Jimrael to see. 'The wet is lost.'

Only at the bottom of the pool was there some damp black mud, where pugs had scraped for the last drops.

'There has been no rain,' said Mr Jimrael. 'And the army has not put the water back into the mountain. But there is water at the well in The Animal Garden. There has always been water.'

'But I know it is here,' said the king. 'I know.' He carefully poured his dry handfuls back into the pool. 'It has gone bad. The water is no use.'

Mr Jimrael had to think about that. 'The water is not getting here at all,' he said.

'It is getting here,' said the king. 'I know. But it has

changed to dry. It will not be drunk. But it is here we must drink.'

'We cannot change his opinion,' said Mr Jimrael. 'Dr Rhamid has said water is here, so it is indeed water, though in a different state. This is not a joke, but a mistake. But what am I telling these poor pugs? I am thinking quickly. I am not used to being God. So now,' he went on, 'all the pugs must drink at the well in The Animal Garden. You are to go there. My goodness, how very exhausting is blasphemy.'

They all looked up at the mountainside. Some way up it, blurred and shimmering in the heat from the rock, stood the grove of dried trees behind their wall.

'There is not enough water to run down to the pool,' said Mr Jimrael. 'That is why the transport was coming. It is not coming now, because the rebels have come down the Pungal River. I do not know what will happen if we cannot get the pugs away. And where are your two fathers?'

The pugs muttered to each other all the way up a path across bare rock, until they were at the gateway in the Garden wall.

Where there should have been the green shade of great trees there was only the sparse foliage of drought, yellow leaves hanging or falling, the shade lying in twigs on the ground.

A lady pug stood in the way, showing the large teeth that had bitten the young pug, guarding the well.

Water trickled out of the cliff face where bushes were still green and there were cool shadows. Water dripped, shiveringly beautiful and tempting. There was a cistern here, a stone tank that should have fed the pool in the city.

There was a new sound in the air. The pugs heard it but it meant nothing to them. Philip looked back to all the parched world of rock and city, and the camp beyond, and the desert beyond that.

From the camp there now rose a plume of smoke. There was a flash of light. Seconds later there was the smack of an explosion, followed by gunfire.

'It is rebels,' said Mr Jimrael. 'One thing and another and sometimes both, dear me. We had better be getting out from here very soon, while there is something to drink.'

Seven

At this time Shanya was having a difficulty. She wanted to take a drink of cool water, but the king of the pugs would not let her get her own. Instead he was getting it for her, in his cupped hands. Now there was real wet water he thought she should drink first. God, of course, could look after himself.

Shanya refused to drink from the pug's hands. In spite of its coolness she was not sure of the water itself.

'It should be thrown away,' she said. 'I cannot go near his paws.'

'I am taking you away,' said Mr Jimrael. 'I think we can get on the road ahead of them, if we are quick and lucky.'

Philip knew there would be a thrilling chase, because he had seen films. They would hurtle round bends, over bushes, through markets, and come directly to safety. There would be a bullet hole in Mr Jimrael's jeep, that would be all.

Mr Jimrael looked at him. He understood Philip's thoughts. 'I do not know what it will be like,' he said.

'But I am not staying here without you,' said Shanya. She could hear guns being fired, and see flames leaping up, and new smokes. They could all see those things. Only the pugs thought they were the usual way men behaved.

'I shall not be useful here, thank you,' said Mr Jimrael, pleased that Shanya spoke at last, and that he was wanted. 'Well, perhaps we should wait a little.'

The king drank his handful of water. He looked puzzled at the way Shanya had treated him. 'Doctor Rhamid has not told his mother the things he has told us about water,' he said.

'You are in their kingdom now,' said Mr Jimrael. Philip knew something had to be done, and went to take water himself. The girl pug in charge of the well opened her mouth at him, but the king dipped his hands again and held water up. Philip put his lips in and sucked the water. After all, the king's hands were as clean as his own.

They waited a little, shaded by bushes, and watched the camp. More pugs walked up from the city, not sure they were doing the right thing. They were allowed to drink. Shanya gathered her clothes round her in case a scrambling infant climbed on her.

The sun went further round the sky. The shadows shifted a very little. At the camp smoke stopped billowing, and lay close to the ground. There were no more noises.

'I think it is time to go,' said Mr Jimrael. 'The rebels will have left. They have burnt the camp and there is nothing for them. But we shall go cautiously. If you want to stay you will be quite safe with the pugs. I can send government soldiers for you.'

Shanya sat tight. She was not being obtuse, or sulking. She felt it would be better to stay among pugs with dirty paws than among rebels with guns. But it was clear she would rather do neither.

Mr Jimrael talked to them both a little longer, telling them about the pugs and where they had come from. 'They cannot tell you themselves, because they do not know.'

The pugs were discovered by Dr Rhamid and were a species new to science. He had named them after himself, which was quite proper, *Papio Rhamidus* in scientific languages, and Pug, from a Scottish poem.

The first pugs had been dead when they were found, on a hill top in a valley being flooded for a reservoir. When he cut them up in the proper scientific manner,

Senjal Rhamid had been interested in their brains and their throats.

'They should be able to speak,' he told his students. 'They have a speech centre and the right shape to their throats. But we may never know, if these are the last two and we have lost all the poems pugs ever made up.'

He was glad to be wrong. The next day live pugs were found on the hill top and captured. They had to be rescued. If they could speak then all they did was swear.

'If you are not rescued you will drown,' Dr Rhamid told them. 'Yess, drown.'

'Yesssssdroon,' said one of them. And Dr Rhamid's neck went prickly with delight at finding the first talking mammal.

He would not let them go to a zoo. He would not let them be separated. He let them free in a big enclosure and spoke to his friend Martin Fleming, and they both spoke to the pugs. After a time they had conversations with them, like 'Go. Come. Food. Take your hand out of my pocket,' followed by laughter from the top of a tree.

Then the two scientists spoke to the President, and the President sent a special man to help them. The pugs and the scientists went out into the desert to the ruined city, which was after all next to The Animal Garden.

Also, it was the very place the pugs belonged to. Carvings of their extinct species had been found here. And the forest where they were found was quite the wrong sort of habitat.

There was an accident on the way. Because of it some of the pugs learned to think. Once you can think about tomorrow you can think about anything. But it meant a transplant and tiny wires, and a crown for the best pugs. They could be told things quick and sure, day and night, through the wires, through their ears. Then they could be given their new home.

But now there were rebels in the country, and the rains did not come, and the army did not send water, and one or two other things.

So when Philip shook hands with Mr Jimrael, and Mr Jimrael set off alone walking down to the city from The Animal Garden, they all thought that perhaps the whole scheme was to be of no use.

Especially since rebel soldiers came out of the ruins, pointed guns at Mr Jimrael, and took him away hurriedly. And other soldiers, out of sight, blew up Mr Jimrael's little jeep in the gateway so the green panels of the body flew into the sky and clattered down the city wall.

Shanya's left hand came out and held Philip's right hand. Her right hand held the king's paw.

'Men are cooking,' said the king, seeing the jeep explode. 'Yess. But they will be safe with God.'

Eight

The last of the pugs left in the city ran about shouting. Some used words, others the language of the wilderness. They sniffed rock to find where Mr Jimrael had gone, and came cautiously out into the open.

They made too much noise. A rebel soldier, carrying stuff stolen from the camp, came back with his gun ready.

A mother pug snarled at him in pure wild voice. He put up his gun and fired at her. Her baby fell from her back and screamed.

'Ouff,' said the king, rushing out of the Garden, gathering stones, and careering down the path. It was a rescue, but an attack first. He was a good shot with his stones. The soldier dropped his gun and put his hands to his head. He dropped something else, picked up the gun, and ran away.

The king sent a farewell stone after him, getting the back of his knee, so that he hobbled his way out of sight. The king picked up what he had dropped, came to the fallen baby, picked that up, and hurried with its mother up to the Garden and the well.

'It is hurt,' said the king. 'Yess, certainly, and we do not know what to do. God will take it. But God has gone home with his friends. We do not understand.'

He put the baby on the edge of the cistern. It whimpered and looked at Shanya with big brown eyes, the white showing at the edges with fright and pain. Shanya stared, but did not know what to do.

Philip took the other thing the king had brought. It was the solar lantern. It had a dent from being dropped, but the tubes came on bright, and the indicator said 'Full Charge 20 hours Max'. But the sun itself was Max already, so the lantern could not take any more charge.

Night will come, Philip remembered. But that was a long way off, with no meals in sight to help the long day pass, only the sun charging the whole landscape with pure heat.

'Full chge,' said the king, puzzling over the words on the solar lantern. 'I am reading but I do not know why. It is in the way of seeing.'

One of the pugs caught a furry animal. It thoughtfully tore it up and ate it. Others came to smell its mouth afterwards. A snake came trickling past, turning away when it saw so much company beside the water. The company, Philip and Shanya included, watched it twine away among the rocks like a section of brown road going its brown way. Then one and all let out a sigh of breath, the danger and horror over. 'We are not liking that thing,' said the king. 'It is causing bother in our heads. On its back I am reading, "Snake eat baby pug".'

In spite of what else he carried, the king had with him a piece of metal. When he used both hands he had held it in a foot. He opened his hand to make sure he had it, and then went searching among the rubble below the cliff for the right stone.

'It is time for fire,' he said. 'That is showing what sort of people we are now.' He went rummaging about in fallen twigs, rubbing dry bark to a powder, sending the young boy pug for more wood.

With rock and steel he made sparks in the tinder, and then flames under twigs, and larger wood on top. Smoke went up.

But the sun was hot already. There was nothing to cook. The king could think of tomorrow but not very well of today. And there were things he had not dreamed of.

The rebels had not left the city. When they saw

smoke they came to investigate, fanning out across the rock and coming slowly. A pug that was watching from a tree did not realize they were approaching until a singing bullet leapt from the wall and thudded into the branch he was sitting on.

The rebels laughed when he tumbled down, and stopped advancing carefully. They were not very much afraid of monkeys, and would shoot them from beyond the range of stone-throwing.

The girl pug who looked after the well went to the gate to look. She came back to the top of the Garden and began jumping about, not knowing what to do or where to go. One rebel at a time she might have tackled, but a group was more than she could manage. In the end she went to the back of the bushes and hid out of sight.

The rebels thought they would go away now, and not trouble about chasing monkeys. But their officer came and told them to see who had lit the fire. Shanya knew their language as well as English.

'They will see us,' she said. 'The pugs they will not notice. No one will trouble with them. But us they will capture, and I do not want that. Jayid, yes indeed, but his rebels, no.'

'They are not God,' said the king. 'But they are very big and many. We shall go to another place.'

There was no other place. And down at the foot of the Garden a rebel had slipped in through the gate, hiding himself among the remains of buildings and peering up through the scanty trees.

Pugs were moving away. Shanya was right. The men did not trouble about them. They knew monkeys did not light fires. They were looking for human animals that did.

It was wet in among the bushes. There was muddy moss. But leaves grew all about, and Shanya thought it might be possible to hide. After all, they could not see the pug girl who had already gone in.

She was there, though. She came forward to challenge them. The king showed longer teeth and she moved back. She wriggled back among the rocks of the cliff, where the water ran out an inch or two deep from the dark inside of the mountain.

Down in the Garden there was a shout and the rattle of stones. A man was running and shouting. There was a loud double bang, and a scatter of chips of rock. A gun had been fired and its bullet had hit the cliff a short instant later, breaking off fragments that yowled through the air.

Nine

'She will bite us,' the king was saying. 'It is her duty. She has been told.' He was talking about the girl pug who looked after the water. He had understood when the baby pug had been hurt by a gun, but even now he did not realize that bullets he could only hear might damage him or his people.

The girl pug went back under a damp overhang of cliff, and all at once slid through a black slot right at the back, where the water trickled from the mountain. She looked out again, showing her teeth.

Shanya, without thinking or complaint, put herself through the same narrow hole and disappeared beyond it into a place beyond. Echoes came out. Shanya was used to ayahs. She had a sharp quarrel with the girl pug, and then her face was looking out.

'You will come,' she said. 'Philip and the king. But first the hurt one.'

First went the pug with the injured child. Philip followed, and then the king and more pugs, until the darkness was full of them, splashing in water cold enough to hurt.

Outside a gun was fired again, and men shouted very close by.

'They will see us,' said Shanya. 'Our tracks will show.'

But Philip saw the water running muddy, then clear, and their footprints gone. A moment later he was looking into the eyes of a man, with the man looking back, but not seeing him or the place they had come through. The man turned away. Men called to each other, meaning that the monkeys had gone away, there were no men here, and it was time to return to being rebels.

Philip reckoned the man had been a long time in the sun, and could not see in the shadows of the bushes. For some time he stood back, ankle-deep in cold water, and watched the opening, listening to the world beyond.

The world close to him trickled with water, singing to itself and back to itself.

By instinct, or perhaps by sense, the pugs were all

quiet for a long time. But at last they began to lift their cold feet up and make little pug complaints.

'My feet are night,' said the king.

'Our feet are dead,' said a young pug.

A baby jumped off its mother's back and became cross at the wet and cold water.

The words, the complaints, the splashing, echoed. Philip thought he was in a swimming bath, with the shadows of echoes running round his head.

When he stopped watching outwards he saw inwards. A little light edged its way through the hole they had entered by. They were in a place with straight walls, with columns and pillars holding up a roof, with a flat floor under the seeping water.

'Someone has made this,' he said, looking all round.

'It is part of The Animal Garden,' said Shanya.

'God did it,' said the king. 'Mister Jimrael.'

'Well,' said Philip, 'it was lucky for us it was here.'

The king did not know what he meant. 'Have the men gone?' he asked. 'We go back to our houses. It is our place. Go and look at our places,' he told the young pug.

The young pug went out. A minute later a gun was fired, and a second after that the young pug was back. He had stolen a rebel's dinner, a lump of sticky sweet stuff.

'He is living in the gateway,' he said. 'And more of him in the houses.'

Shanya took the dinner away from him. Philip did not see it for more than a moment. He assumed she would eat it.

He was shivering now, and did not want to eat. The king was shivering beside him. 'I am night all over,' said the king.

Philip kicked over the solar lantern sitting in the water beside him. He put the switch over, and filled the place with light.

Now they all saw the room. It was made of arches and vaults. The walls were panelled between pillars, and each panel was full of carved drawings.

'I will read those,' said the king. 'Writing is the word of God.' He looked at panel after panel. 'I do not know all these words,' he said. 'There are pugs written here. I have been taught to read words and pictures. I can do it, but I cannot tell you how. It is across everything I see, the word of God.'

Philip thought they were carvings of the gods of thousands of years ago, so the king was right about that. But the pictures were of no use now. The king stopped reading.

Philip looked further into the mountain. The room had a floor of water, but twenty arches away the floor

51

rose higher and the water was confined to a ditch. There would be a drier place there, above the ditch. He took the lantern and went to see.

The place was drier but still cold. He climbed some steps and the water was running below him. He thought the air was warmer than it had been.

He turned the lantern down to a glimmer. Twenty hours of Max was less than a day, but he knew a solar lantern could run for more than a week at a low setting.

I can starve for a few days, he thought. Shanya has taken the food.

The king joined him on the dry floor. 'There are trees in my nose,' he said, sniffing. 'There are no trees like that at our houses now. If there were we could eat.'

'Sometimes,' said Shanya, joining them to be near the light, 'I smell the forest.' She was carrying the wounded baby pug, shawled up in her clothes. She sat down next to the king without shrinking away in disgust, and looked at him as a wise equal.

Ten

Other pugs were floundering in the ditch of water, making noises and sometimes speaking. One of them came out with a great splashing thing, a tree branch with its leaves green and new.

Underground trees, Philip thought. I did not know.

Another spoke in pure pug language and brought a fine fat fish on to the bank and stood with a foot on it, and its mouth open to keep the rest away.

Not, Philip thought, an underground fish, because those are white. This is a river fish that has come in here from a river.

They had all got in here where water came out. Perhaps they could get out again where water came in.

He was trying to explain this idea to Shanya and the king when a great noise began to happen at the place where they had come in. A dim light had been showing there, but that was brushed over with darkness, coming and going. There was a shout inside the underground room, followed by a quiet that was not perfect. There was something more than the running of water.

There was a rippling of the water, a quivering of the ground, and the roar of an engine. A large thing began to push at the hole, at the mountainside round it, and to force its way in.

It rammed and battered, retreated and began to come forward again. It was a tank, treading its way into the mountain.

'They are looking for us,' said Philip.

'We are to be prisoners,' said Shanya.

'But there is a way out,' said Philip. 'If a tree comes in, that is the way out.'

They had to shout between bursts of engine noise.

'But why do they need a tank?' said Philip.

'Rebels think tanks are best,' said Shanya. 'We have had rebellions before. They steal tanks and radios and wine, and the President wins. He is a friend of my father, Professor Rhamid.'

'I am a friend of God,' said the king.

They had this conversation as they walked. The pug with the fish tucked it under his arm and came with them. They went into the darkness in a troupe.

At the mouth of the cave the tank parked itself

now against one side, now against the other, until with a tearing thud something in it broke, and there was shouting instead.

There was also darkness. The way they had come in was tightly blocked.

The way ahead began to change too. The elaborate walls drew close together and changed to being plain rock. But this was not a natural cave. This passage had been cut. Chisel marks still showed, and now and then masonry had filled a gap.

They walked on a sort of towpath beside the water.

The water itself began to rise higher and move faster, as if more and more of it was heaped up somewhere ahead. Then water was over the path, tugging at their feet, trying to take the lighter pugs away. They very sensibly held each others' tails.

Shanya had the wounded baby slung round her neck. The mother held one hand, the king held the other. Philip had two to help him as well, one of them jostling with the solar lantern.

The water began to swirl higher and more fiercely. Looking back Philip saw the long passage full from side to side, and the same ahead, cut off by a curve.

Round the curve they were saved by something unexpected. At first Philip thought it was a dead end to the path, where a wall was built across it. But up the side there was a stairway, up to a higher path.

The air was warmer. At times it wanted to choke in Philip's throat.

'We are coming to the trees,' said the king. 'Where we lived before we were visited by God. It is all God, this life.'

Shanya sat down. 'Turn up the light,' she said. 'It is time for something to eat. The fish. Give me the fish.'

She got the fish. 'It is to be shared out,' she said. The pugs were not sure about that.

'But he caught it,' said the king.

'We shall eat this one,' said Shanya. 'He will catch another.'

The pug looked at the river down in its cleft and was very doubtful. 'Fish will catch pug,' it said. The water ran fiercely in its ditch.

Shanya was in charge, though. The king pulled the fish apart, and it was shared out somehow, and eaten. Shanya rinsed her hands in a puddle and broke up the lump of sticky, sweet, rebel dinner.

Philip spat out a scale of fish and sucked the sweetness.

'It is eaten,' said the king, after a time. He went down the stairs and came up again with something in his hands. He held them out to Shanya.

This time she bent her head and drank from the water in the hands.

They sat where they were. No one wanted to go any further. Philip turned the solar lantern off, and they had night-time, rather wet and not very warm, huddled in a heap.

Philip woke into darkness and a panic he could feel but not hear, the pugs climbing upon one another and on him, trying to get away from something they knew about, invisible, on the ground among them, walking through, treading them down. Its skin was smooth and sharp and its back was long, and swayed from side to side.

Eleven

The lantern was under this thing. Philip had the handle at his fingertips, but could not pull it out. The thing's leg raked him with its claws as it marched. The thing's smell was of dead and rotten stuff.

The weight of its foot pressed Philip to the ground. Then the pressure of its swinging tail held him down. But he had the lantern now, and felt for the switch. Light burst from it, and the pugs saw what had alarmed them.

Now they were terrified and ran in all directions. The long-ridged and knobbed back of a river crocodile went on its way, the splayed legs wallowing it along. It turned its head to look at the light, and turned away again. Its mouth was closed. The jaws had not been seeking prey but warmth in the river of night.

It slid into the racing water and could be seen no

more. Shanya gathered up her baby pug, looked for the mother, and spoke to Philip. He could hear nothing above the water and its clamouring echo.

Shanya knew what she was doing. She used a sort of motherly sense to calm the whole troupe of pugs, and to calm Philip too. There was, after all, something to be learnt from ayahs.

Philip's knees needed calming, because they wanted to walk in different directions from his legs.

Shanya led on a little way until she came to a lump of rock fallen from the roof high above. She sat down on it, wrapped her robes round her, and became still. Philip sat beside her. They could not exchange words, but she took his arm and squeezed it slowly again and again, nodding her head gently as she did so, leading his muscles into calm and rest again.

The king came and considered them, standing up and alert. He was of course watched by the other pugs. They came close too. When he sat down they sat too. When he put a hand on Shanya's foot they put their hands on their neighbour.

Philip began to count on his fingers, to show Shanya he was wondering how many of them were left, whether any had fallen in the water or run away too far. There were twenty people: eighteen pugs, and two humans.

Philip turned down the light as far as it would go without being off. The pugs shuffled closer. One or two began to scratch themselves, a sign that they were less alarmed.

In the end Philip knew they had to stop sitting there in this deaf and dumb fashion. He stood up and led them on.

He needed more light now, because the going was very rough for him and Shanya. The pugs could use all four feet to run over the boulders that littered the way, but humans with two feet and babies and lanterns to carry had to be cautious.

They were no longer merely in a tunnel, but in a cave, wide and high, an underground surface with hills in it, and the water a river among those hills. Philip led them away from the water and out of its noise. He was more comfortable when he could hear his feet kicking loose stones. It was drier further from the water, but boulders were just as large and close together.

The king plucked at his arm and wanted him to look at something. He did not know about pointing, and had to stare in the right direction, flick his head to see that Philip was doing the same thing, and stare again, flick and stare, flick and stare. Until Philip saw what was to be seen.

High in the side of the cave, beyond the river, there

was a patch of light. At first it was only light on rock. But when they had walked further they saw daylight itself, and the sky beyond. Water dripped from this window in a strangely lumpy way.

There was no way of getting there. The side of the cave hung over to make the roof, and the window was in the roof, like a skylight.

It was just as well. Above the noise of the river there were other sounds. A shriek, somewhere between a scream and a yell, went round the cave. Something came running out of that skylight under the roof and hung on the wall. It was tall, white, and strong. It shouted at them, something of a bark, almost words, walking up and down, not glad to see them.

It threw rocks into the water. They splashed and sank. But some of what it threw was lumpy water.

The lumpy water floated. Pieces of it had been washed up in a little bay. The lumps were ice, a form of water that was another form of rock and very puzzling to the pugs – they had never come across melting rock of any sort. Some of them picked up ordinary stones and tried to squeeze and warm them into something to drink.

'But,' said Shanya, 'there is a whole river to drink.'

'They are being scientists,' said Philip. 'Experimenting.'

Air came warm into the cave. It smelt of hillsides with fir trees. The warm air had melted some mountain glacier, some eternal snow, and now stirred round the cavern.

What lived up there lived in that snow, those frosts. What was throwing snow?

'I have heard of things on the mountains,' said Philip.

'Wild men of the snow,' said Shanya. 'A story.'

'But we have seen them,' said Philip.

Shanya did not believe that.

The pugs played with ice and stones. They shouted up at the creature high above.

The striding thing on the wall sent a last animal curse, and scuttled like a huge spider up the wall, across the top, and out into the hillside beyond. It had not dared come down – there was only one way to do so, to jump, and none at all to get back.

That counted as a victory for the pugs.

'King,' said the king, meaning he was still the leader by winning. 'That was not God.'

There were more windows like this one, high on the top of the cave. The next one was there at night, and beyond it, or perhaps just inside, some creature howled, and a bird hooted, and something very wild honked. At one of them, by daylight, a tree grew close outside. Philip thought he saw the bird in its branches looking down the hole in the mountain for a worm or child or pug.

The roof of the cave went up and up, and the river stayed low. They heard themselves speaking, saying what they all knew, that they were cold and hungry, weary and afraid, for a day and a night, and a day and a night.

'Pug's feet are night,' said the king. He meant they were cold.

'I have a pain of hunger,' said Shanya. 'It is like a fishbone in my heart.'

Round a corner, out of the noise of hastening water, with something like sunlight coming on them from high openings, feeling glad of those things, they came across something like heaven.

But of course nothing to do with Mr Jimrael, even if he was God. But it was something they might have rejoiced about even without being cold, lost, and starving, and all alone together.

Twelve

What they had found made the pugs look about suspiciously and cautiously. They fingered something that lay in a heap on the floor of the cave. They grunted. They said words they did not know, but which might mean something.

'We have seen this,' said the king. 'And it hurts.'

Other pugs looked round, they listened, they looked up. They were ready to run. They even whimpered a bit, as if they were already hurt. Their eyes showed white.

They licked their fingers, and forgot about danger. They picked things from the floor of the cave and put them in their mouths.

'They are eating stones,' said Shanya. 'What are they doing?'

Philip did not know. He thought he could smell

something he almost knew. Pugs were eating, but looking round anxiously. They expected something to go wrong.

'They look as if they are being naughty,' said Shanya. 'And will be in great trouble.'

The king stopped filling his mouth. He searched for a stone, or whatever it was, that would suit his purpose. He spoke to another pug, the mother of the baby Shanya was carrying.

Each of them chose something from the ground. The king brought his to Philip. That mother pug brought hers to Shanya.

A day ago Shanya would not have touched what she was brought, if it had been on the floor, or touched by a pug.

But now she was glad to take sticky honeycomb, crystallized and crunchy in its wax, and bite it.

Philip was as glad as she was to taste the sweetness, and feel he was having a meal.

Now both he and Shanya knew what troubled the pugs. Wherever they had lived before, taking honey from the bees had meant being stung. Now they had the honey, but not the stings.

The wounded baby sucked at Shanya's fingers and reached for more, until its hurt shoulder hurt, and it had to be kissed by its mother and by Shanya.

Philip ate his lump of comb, and found another for himself. By the time he had eaten enough he was feeling better. He felt well enough to feel slightly sickened by the cloying delightful stuff.

Far overhead, invisible in a crack, the nest of the bees hummed gently. There was light up there, coming in from another of the high windows, angling brightly across, but not quite a sunbeam.

Honeycomb had fallen from the high nest in that crevice, and lay scattered in round combs like pouches, dark as stone, rich as toffee, sweet and brown.

The pugs were going to eat as much as they could. Philip and Shanya left the heap of fallen combs, because the smell was too strong now they had had enough. They sat for a time licking their fingers and wondering what meal they had eaten and what time of day it was.

Perhaps it was moonlight overhead, Philip thought. Shanya sat silent. The baby slept. One by one the pugs were full, and came away, licking and grooming themselves and one another, yawning and belching.

'It is the afternoon,' said Shanya. 'We are doing nothing. It is a rest. The ayah will be asleep, and perhaps I am thinking of a trick to play on her. Perhaps I am asleep too.'

Shanya told him a sleepy story with lots of gaps about a little dog she once had, and how the ayah had not

66

liked it, and had got rid of it. And then told Shanya they had both eaten it for supper. Shanya had been horrified, but amused at the same time.

Philip was sleepy too, and now no longer felt sick. He missed some bits of the story, and Shanya told it in a muddled way. Philip felt slightly safe now, though not completely so; but there was time to rest, and no need to attend to every sound that came to his ears. He had had honey, and did not want little dog.

Beside him the king scratched his own head, his claws scraping on the golden crown that was part of his head. He went for more honeycomb, brought some back to suck, then dropped it, laid his head against Philip, and went to sleep.

Round them the pugs found real rocks to lean on, and fell silent too. Little whimpers from babies were instantly silenced by a sugary finger, and there were sucking noises.

Overhead the bees fell silent. Only the water, dark in the darkness, rippled and spoke, and a far wind overhead walked gently in the mountains.

It had been a very severe accident, Mr Jimrael had told Philip and Shanya, back in the dry, hot, city. The pugs were being brought into safety, all asleep in cages, tranquillized, when the wagon had slipped on a mountain road, running back to the edge. Two cages had toppled off the back and down the hill.

Dr Rhamid had been frantic about that. There were fewer than twenty of this new species, and two more would now be dead, adding to the ones he had already examined.

He had gone down the hillside himself and brought the two pugs up in his arms, and taken them in his own car to town. He had wept as he did it, Mr Jimrael said.

The two pugs were not dead, but their heads were hurt. Dr Rhamid had had to fashion new bones for them, and mend the precious brains inside. He had to set them working again.

He had taken over the hospital.

He had watched from beyond the glass, while people waited for their own operations.

After all, said Mr Jimrael, there were very many people already in the world, but only eighteen pugs. Who can tell what is completely right?

But Shanya had walked away before that and did not hear it. Philip thought she did not want to know about pugs. Now he thought she had not wanted to show her distress, or wonder whether her father had been right.

There had been no selfish experiment by Dr Rhamid, only a hope to keep the creatures alive and active. In the end he had mended them better than they had been, because, he explained to Mr Jimrael, he could not mend them worse, of course. The only way to keep them alive was to improve them.

Maybe it was evolution, Mr Jimrael had said. He was not God, but he had heard that God moved in mysterious ways. Perhaps Dr Rhamid had been a cause of evolution.

But neither he nor Philip had said anything about that to Shanya.

'I am glad they are here,' said Shanya, when people and pugs began to wake, when some dazzle of sunlight hung high above the break in the roof, when bees began their housekeeping, and to venture speck by speck against the dazzle, first black, then glows of light themselves. 'I would have been lonely just with you, Philip.'

The king thought about this. 'Pugs,' he said, 'are being lonely without you.'

Shanya rubbed her eyes, because she thought about her father. Now she had honey on her cheeks, she said, and her tongue could not reach it, please do not watch, Philip.

Philip had honey between his fingers, making them sticky and slippery at the same time, wax and sweetness that would not lick away.

They went to the edge of the water to wash hands and faces, and to drink. Shanya left the baby with its mother, and brought her a drink in her cupped hands. That, after all, was the best of pug manners.

When Shanya came back to the water Philip thought she had found another baby by the water's edge. She was picking up a bundle, and water was dripping heavy from it. But Shanya knew at once which way up it should be, and had it by the scruff of its neck, as you hold kittens or puppies and probably pugs.

'Philip,' said Shanya, and her voice trembled, 'see what I am finding.'

Then for a time she could not speak at all.

She had found a man's jacket, and was holding it by the collar. Water was draining out of the wool. Even in the bleak light of the cave bottom the pattern of the tweed could be seen, the large red, green, and blue tartan of Dr Rhamid's jacket, that he had worn when he came to the Land Rover, and at the supper table that night at the camp. In it he had been eating and drinking and laughing, making Shanya smile, giggle, and once, even choke.

Now she choked a little again, then drew a breath, and said, 'We must be quite sure. I hope it is not Jayid's fault. I do not know what I will do.'

Philip thought she was going to tear her own clothes,

because she put both her hands to her neck. But she let go of the cloth, sniffed because her nose ran, and began to look more closely at the jacket.

In its pocket was a wallet, a credit card, and money, useless under the ground. The credit card had Senjal Rhamid's name on. They read it by the light straining in from above, bee-flash by bee-flash, and letter by letter in European alphabet.

'If he has lost it, we have found it,' said Shanya.

'We will give it back,' said Philip.

'Yes,' said Shanya, after a little pause. 'Of course we shall do that.'

Peering at a wet page inside the wallet, she found a letter not yet posted. It had been written to her, she said. But the writing was of a kind Philip did not know, the alien signs of Shanya's language, far from the alphabet Philip knew. The stamp was loose on the envelope, and the ink had run like black blood.

Thirteen

'The camp is a long way from the Post Office,' said Philip. Of course that was true, but not a useful or sensible remark.

'The coat is showing he is dead,' said Shanya. 'But you do not care.' She opened another pocket and found computer disks in plastic envelopes, the labels soft as porridge. She squeezed the sleeve and smelt at it, as a pug would do.

The king came to see what they had found. He did not come in a great hurry, being full of honey. He took a sniff too.

'The good Doctor Rhamid is close by,' he said. 'Yess. We are finding him soon. Oh God, he will say, and there is Mister Jimrael.'

'You are dreaming,' said Shanya.

'It is still nearly night,' said the king. Now he

thought of night he thought of cold as well, and wanted to make a fire, since the day down here could never be warm. The king could make sparks, but there was nothing to catch them on, nothing to burn.

All the same, Philip's nose wanted to smell smoke, and thought it did. But he knew as well it was Dr Rhamid's jacket, all the way from a weaver's hut in the mountains that smelt of burning cedar for ever.

Only, of course, he had not put his nose on the prickly wet cloth.

The light from outside went away. He turned up the solar lantern, and they used that for a camp fire.

'He is dead,' said Shanya, thinking of her father. She said it to make finding him an even greater joy, if it happened. A coat is not the whole person: sometimes it is better, sometimes it is worse.

After some time the pugs were restless. They did not want more honey, but were hungry for something else. They were lifting their noses and sniffing at air that was sometimes warm, sometimes cold, moving above their heads.

'It is men,' said the king. 'Pugs are afraid of men. They have forgotten they are now men themselves. Doctor Rhamid has told us so. If we are good, he says, yess. But pugs are not hungry for good. They have never seen it growing on the tree.'

'They think men are like my father,' said Shanya. 'But they are not all.'

'Or like Mr Jimrael,' said Philip.

'I am wondering whether he is a shopkeeper,' said Shanya. 'But shopkeepers are not also God. It is a puzzle.'

'He is not God either,' said Philip.

'The world is a shop,' said Shanya, 'if God is a shopkeeper. I do not think that, but I will tell my ayah and torment her.'

They walked on by lantern-light, the cave floor rising under them, the water always trickling not far away.

There was something like a broken bridge against the wall of the cave, its girders propped and joined. The pugs had no curiosity about it, but Philip had to stay and look at the skeleton of something larger than an elephant, slumped and leaning, the head with its tusks on a pillow of rock, the bones furred with moss. It had thousands of years ago been caught in the cave, and died here. Philip thought of twenty skeletons, he and Shanya and eighteen pugs, fossilizing for ever beside it.

There was an underground hillside to climb up. Water cascaded down beside them, and then under their feet. But at the top of the slope, where the roof came down low, which sky never does, the air

74

thickened and smelt of the world outside.

Stone was overhead still, or darkness as blank as stone, and no stars shone. But Philip wondered, over the babble of the water, whether he heard wind caught in trees, or perhaps a greater stream of water not far away but in some other room.

The pugs became uneasy. They began to look alarmed, to bark softly to one another, to show their teeth.

'What do they mean?' Philip asked the king. The king was sharing the alarm and was unable to speak. He was once again only an instinctive *Papio Rhamidus* among his tribe. Philip was the one who could not speak or understand what was truly obvious.

At the top of this slope of stone they had come across others.

Now there was more light than lantern-light. There were flames ahead, and shadows moving by the flames. The shadows were people walking, projected on the ground, or sometimes huge on a cave wall.

'We are outside,' said Shanya. Philip saw that the shadows were on the cave roof still.

Shanya had more to say. 'It is rebels, perhaps,' she whispered. 'Jayid lived in a cave before he made a rebellion.' She was not alarmed at the thought of Jayid.

75

By now it was too late to do anything. Philip, Shanya, and the pugs could not choose to go back. People had heard them coming long before, and were already behind them, rattling stones but staying in hiding.

'We shall be dead too,' said Shanya, her voice squeaking. She held the king's hand. Philip kept his own hand away, because he wanted to walk forward. Sometimes it is best to be brave when there is nothing else to be done. Then it is necessary.

The pugs clustered round Shanya and the king. Philip stepped away from them, held the lantern up high, and turned it to its full power. It was very bright. Light shone all round, there were few shadows, and the cave walls showed like the boundary of the world.

'Who is there?' said Philip, not quite so loud and firm as he liked. It is what you say to bandits in the garden when all the staff of your bungalow are asleep. 'My men are pointing guns at you.' He said it in English. Then he repeated it in the language of the country. When he had said the words, and nothing happened, he became very frightened. He had nothing else to do or say, and the bandits might know.

He held the lantern above his head, and looked round, trying to appear calm.

'Is it Jayid?' he asked, after a little practice with a reluctant voice. 'Is Jayid here?'

'Sir,' said a voice, quietly, 'we are only women and children here, please. Do not be harming us. We are running away from Jayid and the government soldiers, and we are greatly in fear in this place, and much more so before we ventured to come in.'

'We are trying to come out of the mountain,' said Shanya. 'We are women and children too, and I am carrying a little hurt beast.'

'We are lost,' said Philip, lowering the lantern, because it weighed two and a half kilos and his arms were wobbly anyway, and turning the brilliance down.

The king came and took it from him, squatted on his haunches, looked round, and said to the woman, 'We are looking for God, yess. Have you been seeing him about?'

Fourteen

Philip took the lantern back from the king and switched it right off. It was like switching the darkness on, and his eyes stayed thick with coloured shadows.

But the pugs could no longer see. They were still alarmed, and had begun picking up the stones. Now they had nowhere to throw them. If you surround a band of pugs they want to fight back.

'Go to one side,' Shanya was saying to the women of the cave. 'You are frightening these people. These are the people of God.'

'Yess,' said the king. 'And God will be angry with us. Put on the day. Why are you having night?'

Philip put the lantern on at a low setting. The women of the cave were now pallid faces with bright eyes, clustering together, holding their little children. Little children had huge eyes. Big ones round about had theirs narrowed and focussed. Their hands held stones.

The king dropped his stone. 'This world is wrong,' he said. 'There are more people than pugs, oah, yess. How can that be?'

It was not easy to explain. The king saw eyes, eyes of humans, showing alarm by showing the white parts. So many of them, and so alarmed, made the pugs nervous.

The baby in Shanya's arms whimpered. One of the women came forward. 'You have a baby?' she asked. 'From out of the mountain? Is it hurt?'

'I do not know how to look after it,' said Shanya. 'The rebels shot it.'

The woman said that Jayid was outside, but in the mountains. She thought they would all be shot, and there was no safe place in the world. She and her friends and their children had come into the caves for safety.

She told the older children in her own language to put down their weapons of stones, and they relaxed, but stayed watchful.

At first the women had thought the pugs were ghosts, which frightened them in ways they understood. This woman was even more alarmed at the way they spoke English in whispery voices, but thought she might be able to explain that.

She bravely ventured to look among them for her grandfather, because he had been a ghost for years now

79

but never came visiting. She would tell him what she thought of that, she said, not carrying out his duty. He had known English, she said, from the army.

Then there were barks, and showing of teeth, and some snaps of temper, by tired pugs and frightened women and children who had had nothing to do for a week or more except sit by a fire and wonder where the sun had gone. Now they had dropped their stones noisily, to show who was in charge, even without fighting.

'It is boys being men,' said the woman.

'It is the same with pugs,' said Shanya. They both nodded their heads wisely.

The baby was examined by several women, and its mother took another look after that.

Philip was left out of things. He had the lantern, but he himself was only another child among many. He had to hold the lantern tight, or a bigger child would have taken it.

The king took over the campfire. That was his speciality. He remembered lighting it, back in the city of fountains, but did not know how it had got here. He looked for his lizard, because that went with the fire and was not here either.

The women had other food. There was not much, but they insisted on sharing it. The pugs insisted too, because food does not belong to anyone until it is in your own paw. They shared towards themselves, not with others.

Philip wanted to think what to do next, how to deal with women and children, and get on their way. All he could do now was hold on to the lantern. He switched it off and watched the flames of the fire. The king leaned against him. I will wake him up, Philip thought, in a moment, and tell him he is snoring.

The whole world went quiet round him, switched off. Then he wondered why he was dreaming of trains, and knew he was asleep.

When people began moving about he found it must be morning. There was tea to drink, and the pugs were looking across darkness to a white path that led to a white door.

'It is the lake,' said the women. 'We came in here across the lake. That light is day shining across the water, but we dare not go out into the world. We are all ghosts now.'

'It is water,' said the king. 'There is a Land Rover talking across there.' There was an engine roaring somewhere.

'We cannot swim,' said Philip. He knew he had to cross the lake and get to the Land Rover. The king would be right about the Land Rover, he told

Shanya. After all, pugs had been in it.

'It is anybody's Land Rover,' said Shanya. 'Pugs do not understand there are other ones – they only see one of each thing, or very great many.' She was bandaging the baby, with the help of one of the women and anxiety from the mother. All pugs know that if you wrap someone up it is because you are about to eat it.

The women had come across the water on rafts, they told Philip. They had used some of the rafts for firewood, but two were left. The children and the ghosts must take them, they said. When they had pushed them across with poles they would float back. They had floated here. Much wood had floated here, and a dead antelope. They had eaten that.

'We shall go ahead, and you will follow us,' said Philip.

'You will be safe with me,' said Shanya. 'Safe from the government and from the rebels, from Jayid.'

She's so certain, bossy, sure, thought Philip. And she's wrong. But we must get out of here.

There was trouble about that with some of the pugs. They did not want to ride in the Land Rover again, the king said, and the raft made them uneasy. They climbed on it, and climbed off. Several of them said they would float across on some nice steady rocks they could trust; and they rolled their eyes to show their uncertainty.

82

It seemed to take half a day to get them settled. Everybody ended cold and wet, and usually cross.

It was difficult for Philip to get back on land to give the women the only gift he had. He had to explain hurriedly, in a language he did not know at all well, how to use the solar lantern, and gave it to the one most in charge. She hung it firmly on her arm.

'It will outlive us,' she said, her hands together and thanking him for a kindness that could be no real use if they all died.

None of the pugs had any idea about helping to use a pole to punt across with. They sat and watched Philip. Only the little ones, bigger than babies, thought it was fun to climb up the pole Philip was using and jump off the top of his head and run up the pole again.

'It is a circus,' said Shanya. She slapped an excited infant.

Philip poled the raft. It went right and left of the shining reflection that made a path in the water. The current dragged on the pole and twisted the raft. But always it went towards the origin of the reflection, the light itself that came from outside.

Pugs could see each other now in the increasing light. Philip saw that Shanya was looking very untidy, and had a dirty face. She also had a tartan jacket draped wetly on her shoulders.

Somewhere men shouted. The light they were heading for flickered.

Fifteen

The raft was hitting rocks. Pugs complained about that and considered feeling sea-sick. But the raft stayed still, if a little wobbly. They had crossed to the other side, even if they had now to wade to get to dry land.

There was no dry land at first. There was only a stream between cave walls, and a waterfall coming down into the cave. They had to climb that.

At the far side of the underground lake the solar lantern went out. The women had seen they were safely across.

The raft set itself loose when its passengers left it. It made up its own mind where to go, and swirled away there slowly. From this side there was no path of light to the far side, but the raft had no doubts.

Beyond the waterfall there was sky, and daylight, and noises of the outer world.

A threshing noise turned out to be a water buffalo on the edge of some trees. It looked at them piggily, and went back to watching men the other side of it. A scarred shoulder had healed into a white star. One horn had been snapped.

The men were trying to drive it away from this place. The buffalo was thinking about driving the men away, and no one was getting anywhere.

There were other creatures, too. Some were in shadows under trees, some were in the trees, others prowling about openly.

The buffalo was refusing to cross the water and go up the hillside beyond. The water was rising against a rock-fall. The animals were trapped in a piece of forest, and the only way out was where the men tried to drive them.

The whole of this place was in a deep valley. The mountains the pugs had come through rose up this side like a cliff, those the other side hung down from the sky with clouds round their throats and glaciers like jewels glittering beneath their high snows.

And it was raining, raining, rods of water, warm and sticky, hitting hard, again and again. In the peaks lightning flashed and thunder banged the solid rock until it trembled.

A covered truck, though not a Land Rover, was

struggling along a track on the far side. The track was melting under it.

The men were shouting again, but now it was at Shanya and Philip. They forgot the buffalo. The men's clothes were flattened against them and dark with wet. They ran all together towards Philip and the king, Shanya and the mother pug.

The king was drenched and uncomfortable. 'These are not God,' he said. 'Why?'

'They are soldiers,' Shanya shouted above the cannonade of thunder.

The king wanted to throw stones, but there was only mud. Philip had to hold his hands with one of his, and use the other to slow the soldiers down.

However, they were not soldiers, but forest rangers, and they were not capturing but rescuing. They thought the animals were more important than Philip and Shanya. Philip and Shanya should know better than to be here, they shouted.

'They should not speak to me like that,' said Shanya. 'I am carrying the baby pug.'

In the end the rangers stopped rushing and began beckoning, stepping away, understanding what they had come across, excited by finding pugs, having certainly heard of them, and wondering what Philip and Shanya were. One of them went labouring up the hill on all fours, like a pug himself, hurrying, hurrying.

Beyond the trees there was water, at first with trees in it, then yellow hillside all washed down into mud and gritty shale. Then there was the bare rock hillside itself, running underfoot with rain, drowned overhead with it, water pounding, beating, and bruising, rising to meet the rain. The rain still came down like bright steel rods.

It was easier travelling for the pugs, but they were wretched with water, sneezing as it ran into their snouts, shaking their heads as it entered their ears, only to find that cold water now ran into their under-coats and chilled their skin.

Just as it became impossible to travel any further, because the weight of rain and the fierce slope became too much, real soldiers appeared, water running from their guns but their muscles big and fresh.

They stopped short when they saw the pugs, but their officer told them to bring the whole party along smartly.

Weary pugs were glad to hold hands, be taken up to the road and did not object to being bundled into the truck with a canvas roof. They shook and shivered, and made faces at the men.

'Take me to God,' said the king. The soldiers looked

at one another, told each other it was true, and that it could not be.

Philip and Shanya went in with the pugs. I am a pug, Philip thought. The soldiers think I am.

The soldiers put up the backboard of the truck, climbed into the cab, and drove off.

'Are they rebels?' Philip asked.

'They are the President's men,' said Shanya. She unwrapped the baby, who was the driest of them all. It had been in Dr Rhamid's tweed jacket, reading his credit card. 'They will find my father.' She took the credit card away and gave the baby the letter to read. It licked the stamp and then could not find it on the end of its nose.

It is funny, thought Philip. But pugs do not understand funny at all.

One of the others took the stamp and ate it solemnly, then spat it out.

Down in the bottom of the valley the tag of forest was becoming smaller. The buffalo was now defending it by charging at the forest rangers if they came at all near. There was certainly a black bear ready to start a fight too, and some other creature snarling and spitting.

The truck went up the mountain road, spraying out a yellow wake behind it, yellow floods washing its windscreen, mud flowing over its roof. Now and then it slipped on the road. Philip waited for it to roll down the slope.

Worse than thunder, a huge helicopter, a Chinook with two rotors, climbed up the valley beside them, and went ahead, lights flashing from it, its banging engines shaking earth and sky.

When it had gone a wave of water ran reckless and wild down the valley, boiling over the forest with the buffalo and the other animals. On the slope above the forest rangers clung to rocks and stumps and watched helplessly.

Sixteen

There was an army camp round the next curve, canvas grey with water, the ground yellow with mountain clay. The view from the back of the truck swung to one side, and there were cedar trees. Under the trees were men with guns, and drooping tents in rows. The truck stopped. One of the men began to explain to an officer, and the rest went away.

The helicopter had settled into a clear space in front of a large square tent or marquee. Men were going into the marquee, some in army uniforms that had turned dark as the rain soaked them. Others were draped in sacks. There was a lot of shouting.

Pugs began to lean out from the truck and look at the ground. They began to climb up and sit on the tilt. Some thought of getting to the cab and going for a drive, because the weather must be better somewhere else, Philip thought. They began to jump off and go up into the trees.

Men came out of the big tent. How strange they look, Philip thought. Pugs are more normal for me now.

One of the men was in his shirtsleeves, and was angry. Soldiers were trying to calm him down. He pushed one of them away, who had taken his elbow. The soldier pushed back.

'Take care of the baby,' said Shanya, putting a bundle of shawl and pug into Philip's lap. She was trying to climb out over the backboard of the truck, and her clothes were catching on the latches and hooks. She unwound herself suddenly, and left her long robe hanging and did not care.

She went away among the trees with her head uncovered, wearing pink and green Bermuda shorts and a yellow T-shirt with 'I ♥ Malumar Jayid' written on it. Round her shoulders she had put the tweed jacket, now rather puggified and dirty. She was not at all any of the Shanyas that Philip had known so far.

He could see what would happen as it took place. If you walk among the President's soldiers wearing a T-shirt that says you love the rebel leader, the soldiers point guns at you. They also shout.

Philip did not expect the next bit, that the angry man

in shirtsleeves would come running to her, take his jacket from her shoulders and put it on his own, pick her up, rub noses like a pug, put her down again, and without either of them looking back to the truck, lead her into the tent.

The king had climbed to the ground and was looking for twigs for a fire. 'Doctor Rhamid has found his mother,' he said. It was just a fact to him, and meant nothing more.

It meant more to Philip. The baby pug in his arms had staring, sunken, eyes. Its paws were like claws. It had a dry, open, mouth, and its little teeth had never been used. Philip thought they never would be. No wonder it had not been able to read Shanya's letter, no wonder it had not even eaten the stamp, or found it on its nose. It was a sick baby pug. The mother looked at it. She thought the same, and looked away. She had given up hope. 'Pug,' she said. 'Pug no more.'

But this baby was one of only eighteen pugs in the world and it had to be more again.

'Come on,' he said firmly to the mother, and took her by the hand as he climbed to the ground himself. She followed, knowing it was a waste of time.

Philip had nothing written on his shirt except pug dribble, but guns were pointed at him too. That was until he met Dr Rhamid coming from the tent with

Shanya, and held the baby up to him.

He did not hear what Dr Rhamid or Shanya said, because coming next was Mr Jimrael, all smiles and in a wet hat. Behind Mr Jimrael was Dad, his head bandaged, in torn shorts and a soldiery shirt.

There was rubbing of noses and shaking of hands. 'I am on both sides,' said Mr Jimrael. 'You see, the President is my own cousin on my father's side, so I am never out of work. And in case I am, Malumar Jayid is my own cousin on my mother's side. Not of course that I love him, but that is a family thing, not very personal.'

When the rebels captured Mr Jimrael he had told them all this, the rebels had told Jayid, Jayid had told his own men, and Mr Jimrael had been set free.

'They cannot do without me,' he said. 'Not on either side of the affair. And since I am very much indeed interested in the pugs I was able to buy Dr Rhamid and Dr Fleming back from the rebels and bring them here in my own helicopter, and indeed I have paid for Miss Shanya and Master Philip too. But, children, tell me how you came here, complete with the pugs, all by yourselves and wasting my money?'

Then there was some chasing about, shouting, and clicking of guns. The mother pug had gone into the tent and taken a banana. No one minded. In fact they thought it was rather sweet of her. But she then went back, stole the rest, and was eating them quietly to herself when the rest of the pugs thought she should share them.

In the wet and splashy romp that followed the soldiers had made their guns ready. Also the king had decided to build a fire in the back of the truck, and was upset when the army would not listen to his good reasons for doing so. Or even allow themselves to be bitten by the royal teeth.

The king had called on God, God, God, please, to help, and Mr Jimrael had obliged. There was a nice fire not long afterwards on the ground under the trees. Also, the rain stopped, so the soldiers began to wonder about Mr Jimrael being God too, and ending the wet weather.

'It is that exceedingly wicked Professor Rhamid,' said Mr Jimrael. 'Of course I am in charge of all the money for the rescue of the pugs, so I say yes and no for what can be expended. Unfortunately Dr Rhamid is impatiently telling the pugs that I am even more powerful until they are thinking I am God, but it is not so. Only the pugs think that. I am a humble man.'

'I am talking to myself,' said Dr Rhamid. 'That is all. I laugh at my own jokes, yess.'

'He does so,' said Dad. 'I do not listen.'

'I am not religious,' said Dr Rhamid. 'Perhaps I have

been swearing when the pugs are there. Now some people would have said much worse things about Mr Jimrael, who is indeed my very good friend. And of course I have had to tell my pugs how the world came about in the first place. Now they are speaking they must have something to be talking about.'

There were more visitors. The forest rangers came wearily up the hill. They had been unable to save the animals, they said, but they had brought back a file of women and children they had found wandering the mountain with a solar lantern.

Dr Rhamid handed a mended baby back to its mother. Soldiers brought in bowls of rice. And the rain started again, washing mud away from the faces of the cave children.

'Well,' said Mr Jimrael, to show that he did not mind not being all-powerful, 'cleanliness is next to godliness.'

Seventeen

The helicopter had to be made safe for all the passengers. The back part of the cargo hold was divided off for the pugs with a net. The front part held Dr Rhamid, Dr Fleming, Mr Jimrael and soldiers.

'We do not know the situation,' said Mr Jimrael. 'It is best to bring soldiers.'

Shanya and Philip chose to sit with the pugs.

No one could talk while they were flying, because of the noise. Teeth came alive and buzzed against their neighbours. Pugs looked out of the high-up window and worked out how to open the doors.

The soldiers, Dr Rhamid, Mr Jimrael, and Dad, were all sitting on the part of the cargo that was army tents, a generator, food, and fuel for a new camp.

The pugs were nervous and smelly, really wanting to open the doors and get away. The soldiers wrinkled their noses, wishing the same thing. Shanya rubbed the pugs' arms to calm them.

The helicopter swung heavily down the valley. Philip saw how the river, running into the last patch of forest, had burst through fallen rock and left a whirlpool in a hole, with not a single animal rescued, buffalo or bear. 'And a panther,' Mr Jimrael shouted. And Philip nodded.

The machine lifted into cloud. Beyond the cloud it flew among crags and pinnacles, until the snow dried up, the clouds melted, and the desert stretched below, running flat from the dry mountains.

The sun began to hit in through the small windows. The sides of the body became warm. The doors were ready to fly open.

The helicopter landed in a sandstorm it made for itself. The rotors slammed and rocked to a standstill. Everybody was deaf.

Pugs climbed out dizzily and sat on the dry ground, their fur fluffing out dry as if it had been shampooed. It had been close to them in the higher air and nervous places.

Philip felt the sun driving down on him like a drill. A soldier gave him a hat. He warmed himself at the sun, like being too close to a fire. The long cold of the cave was radiated away. He could feel it reaching his bones.

Gradually deafness stopped. The passengers began to hear their own noises, and the sounds of unloading, being reflected back from the city wall almost a mile away, and a second time from the cliff of rock mountain beyond.

Soldiers went to the city to see about rebels. They thought they would have left, because there was no value in a ruined city without water at the end of a road leading nowhere else.

'Bring them back alive,' said their officer, not very loudly.

Mr Jimrael was getting messages on the radio telephone. Jayid had given up, as usual, he said, and gone to live in Singapore. 'That is good.'

'Ah,' said Shanya. 'Until next time.'

'Who knows what side to be on?' said Mr Jimrael.

Soldiers came back from the city with a lot of noise and smoke, riding on the tank the rebels had left and firing into the air. The rebels had not known how to run the tank, and it still worked perfectly. It crunched the remains of Mr Jimrael's jeep, and then stormed across the desert.

The helicopter was emptied of its load. A truck would come in a day or two, to clear the camp and decide where to take the pugs. For the time being they would be in their own cages.

'The delicious experiment has not worked,' said Dr Rhamid. 'But it is not a failure.' He was shaking Mr Jimrael's hand. 'It is only circumstances.'

'We have been beaten by the rainy season,' said Dad. 'It has gone somewhere else once again.'

And the President's soldiers had been too busy with the rebels to bring water to the city. No one had started the pipeline; no one had driven a tanker here.

The blades of the helicopter slashed their way into the sky. It circled, and straightened up for the return journey. Then it abruptly turned again in a narrow loop, and came back to the ground.

'Lie flat,' said Dr Rhamid. 'It is crashing. These things inevitably do, oah yess.'

But the machine landed perfectly well. Its pilot and co-pilot came running from it, though, as if it would explode. However, they were pointing to the city and the mountain, not to the Chinook. Philip did not know what they were saying.

'It is hardly possible,' said Dr Rhamid. 'It is outside reason.'

'It is what we hoped for but could not do,' said Mr Jimrael. 'We must go to the city and see for ourselves.'

The soldiers from the helicopter followed. They all ran to the city wall, through the damaged gateway where Mr Jimrael's jeep had been destroyed not once but twice, and up among the streets. The pugs were here already, looking for homes, scraping the dry pool and finding no drink.

But with a sudden gurgle the pool where the king had showed how the water had dried began to fill again, water welling up from the bottom of it, lifting powdery mud to float on top. The pugs jumped about.

'The water is living again,' said the king, scooping up thin mud and dropping it again. 'Ouf.'

'There is more,' said Dr Rhamid. 'Look.'

They looked up towards The Animal Garden. Through the scanty trees the scar left by the tank was quite obvious, and strangely shiny. All the little green bushes had gone.

In their place water was running, not the shallow trickle of a few days ago, but a brown and steady flood, deep enough to be smooth, gentle enough to shine, though it seemed at times to be carrying boulders and pieces of tree with it.

The pugs went running to see this flow. The girl pug in charge of The Animal Garden was anxious to stay in charge, so there was some clashing of teeth.

But the pugs came running back and scattered all over the bare rock. First there was a flood of water in the gateway of The Animal Garden. On the flood came something else, rolling and angry. A plain black forest cat, a panther, sprang up on the garden wall, shook itself, licked its chest, and twitched its tail.

At the well itself a bear stood up. An antelope stepped on dry rock. Shadows slipped among shadows in the fallen divisions of the Garden, where the wolves had returned.

The water stopped flowing, but only for as long as it took for an angry water buffalo to butt its way through the opening and get on its feet. On its shoulder was a scar like a star, and one horn was broken short.

The animals had returned to The Animal Garden.

And then, with shivering and spurts and bursting noises where blockages cleared, all over the ruined city, fountains dry a thousand years began to rise towards the sky in forgotten squares and plazas and places where streets met.

The king brought Mr Jimrael water in his cupped hands. 'You are most certainly God,' he said. 'Pugs will show you where to live, and you will tell them how. Oh, we will build you a thimble, indeed.'

'A temple?' said Mr Jimrael. 'Oh, I will find one. There are plenty here.'

But he was pleased.

'Thimble,' said Shanya. 'It will be a big one.'

The radio telephone rang. Mr Jimrael listened and handed it to Shanya. 'It is your ayah,' he said.

'But I am busy,' said Shanya, busy being an ayah herself to baby pugs. 'You talk to her.' And she handed the telephone to the king.

After a few sentences he bit off the horrid voice and spat it out.

Acclaim for William Mayne

'The most original writer for children in the land.'
The Times

'. . . a superb, unconventional writer.'
Joanna Carey, *Guardian*

'William Mayne is an astonishing writer.'
Books for Keeps

'. . . probably our most original living
writer for the young.'
The Observer

Another title by William Mayne

THE WORM IN THE WELL

Something touched the backs of his legs, pushing his cloak against him. A thrill like a thread of clear cold steel ran up his back and spread down his arms. His ears heard a sigh round them, his eyes saw the dusk turning solid beside the water, and something slid softly into the water with the smoothest ripple, down into the depths.

She told me, he remembered. She told me not to come. I have, and it cannot be undone.

Granny Shaftoe tried to warn them. A witch she may have been, but she spoke the truth. Meric, proud and fearless, had no time for soothsayers, ignored her wisdom . . . and was never seen again.

Robin missed his friend, and spoke of him often to his son, Alan, and the foundling child Margaret. Before long, these children, too, went deep into the forest to fish from the well. And they met Granny Shaftoe along the way . . .

3 8002 01083 8300

Another title by William Mayne

A SWARM IN MAY

'I don't see why I should be Beekeeper,' Owen thought, 'just because I'm the youngest Singing Boy in the school.'

There has not been a Beekeeper for centuries, though the tradition is still alive. But Owen would rather not take his turn. Until he explores one of the Cathedral towers and finds something to change his mind forever. Solving a mystery which has been baffling people for hundreds of years . . .

'. . . elusive, eliptical, uncompromising . . . I read and re-read it. I wished I had written it, I began to feel almost that I *could* write it. It showed me the way I must go.' Jan Mark, *Books for Keeps*